Thomas, What Do You See?

Author ~ Lori Thomas Hicks
Illustrator ~ Carolyn Overholt Balogh

ISBN (Paperback) 979-8-9913167-0-5
ISBN (Hardback) 979-8-9913167-1-2

Thomas, What Do You See? First published: August 6, 2024
Original date penned as What Do You See?: February 6, 2021

Author's dedication~
To my youngest son for inspiring me to write this book.
Thank you for being a light in this world.

Illustrator's dedication~
To my alter ego: "There is no ending, it's just the place
where you stop the story."   ~Frank Herbert

Thomas is an energetic, busy little boy who loves to run and play. He is going, going, going all day long and rarely slows down for even a moment.

He moves so fast most of the time, he doesn't see what he is missing.

Today is a typical Saturday for Thomas as he is focused on getting outside to play. In the process, he runs straight through the house to his bedroom, without seeing that Grandma has come to visit all the way from Maryland.

When Thomas emerges from his room, his brother tries to get his attention, but Thomas doesn't see him.

As if that wasn't bad enough, Thomas runs outside, picks up his skateboard, and starts zooming up and down the street. He doesn't see his loyal dog, Gus, eagerly watching his every move.

Mama sees that Thomas is missing out on so many special experiences with the people who love him. As she looks up at the puffy clouds in the sky, she gets an idea and decides to intervene.

"Thomas," Mama says, "I'd like you to come with me for a few minutes. I want you to see something."
Begrudgingly, Thomas walks with Mama to the side yard, a little disappointed that he has to stop playing to humor his mama.

Mama sits on the grass, encouraging Thomas to do the same. Thomas is confused at this point, but eventually complies and sits down on the cool grass next to Mama.

"Thomas, I want you to look up and tell me what you see."
At this point, Thomas thinks Mama is being silly and he is slightly annoyed, but he plays along, hoping to get back to skateboarding as soon as possible.

As they both lay on the grass looking up at the puffy clouds in the sky, Mama asks him again, "Thomas, what do you see?"

Thomas replies, "Clouds," with a tone indicating, of course, there is only one possible right answer.

"No, Thomas, what do you see in the clouds?"

Thomas scans the sky for what Mama thinks she
sees. Just then he sees it. It's a cloud shaped
like a turtle right above him.
Thomas shouts with joy. "It's a turtle, Mama.
Do you see it?"

"Yes, Thomas, I see it," Mama responds.
"Sometimes it is important to take the time to see
the amazing things around you."
"Now, Thomas, I think we should go back to the
front of the house," Mama explains, pleased with
the experience they shared.

They walk arm and arm around to the front of the
house, while Thomas watches the turtle fading
into the puffs of white.

Thomas and Mama stand on the sidewalk where
earlier he was riding his skateboard up and down
the street.

Thomas is a little confused because he was on
the front sidewalk when Mama stopped him to
look at the clouds. "Does this mean I can
skateboard now?" he wonders.

Mama gestures toward the house and asks, "Thomas, what do you see?"

Thomas looks around, noticing nothing in particular. "The yard?" he responds, making it more of a question than a statement.

"No, Thomas, what do you see in the yard?" Mama asks.

Gus cannot contain his excitement, so he lets out a series of barks to get Thomas' attention. Thomas sees Gus with his paws on the fence, wagging his tail with enthusiasm, and looking straight at him.

"Gus," Thomas shouts with glee, "Hey boy, whatcha doing?" Thomas pats his faithful friend on the head and says, "I'm sorry I didn't see you. You're such a good boy.

"I see him, too," Mama says in a whisper under her breath as she sees the joy on Thomas' face. "It looks like Gus is really happy you came to see him."

Thomas lets Gus out of the side yard and playfully wrestles with him on the front lawn.

"We're not quite done yet, Thomas," Mama says, "We have one more stop."

Mama makes her way to the living room in the house with Thomas and Gus following closely behind.

"Thomas, what do you see?" Mama asks.

"Our house," Thomas replies, pretty sure he hasn't missed anything this time.

"I see her, too." Mama thinks to herself with a smile that stretches all the way to her heart. She is happy to see Thomas engaged with those that love him so much.

Thomas and Mama sit down at the table and play dominoes with his grandma and brother until close to bedtime.

"No, Thomas, what do you see in the house?"
Mama smiles as her eyes move toward the kitchen table.
Thomas follows his mama's gaze and sees Grandma and his brother sitting at the table playing a game.

"It's Grandma!" Thomas shouts with joy. Thomas runs to Grandma's open arms and gives her the biggest hug he can muster. "I'm so happy to see you, Grandma," Thomas says as they embrace.

Not once did he think about running outside to play.

That night, as Mama tucks Thomas into bed, she asks him very softly, "What do you see, my darling boy?"
Thomas says, "That's an easy one, Mama. I see you."
"And what do you see in me?" Mama asks as she kissed him goodnight.
"I see that you love me," Thomas says, as he drifts off to sleep.

Author's Bio

Lori Thomas Hicks is an accomplished and highly respected educator with thirty-five years of experience as a teacher, administrator, university instructor and educational leader. She has called Paso Robles, California home for nearly three decades. Her life's work has focused on developing systems to support all children, particularly those who are often overlooked or marginalized. She is a loving wife, proud mother, and a doting grandmother; and, it is her family that gives her the greatest inspiration. Lori loves to write about personal experiences, with a twist. *Thomas, What Do You See?* is Lori's second children's book. Her first book is titled, *I Think My Mama Swallowed a Watermelon Seed*.

Illustrator's Bio

As an artist and teacher, Carolyn Overholt Balogh revels in the exploits of adventure and the spirit of curiosity and learning. She lives on the central coast of California with her husband, their active dog and arthritic kitty. She painted these illustrations virtually on Photoshop, which was a first for her, and a bit like wrangling a herd of cats in the sky. This is the second children's book she has illustrated with the author, Lori Thomas Hicks.